Dr. Goldilocks and Bears Fight COVID-19

Edward Gale Movius, MD, FACP, FACE
Illustrated by Kayla Victoria Byrnes

Edward G. Movius MD

In memory of my beloved wife, Therese Georgiana Brendler, Ph.D., a loving mother, a gifted microbiologist and scientist, a dedicated science teacher and mentor to young women scientists, and a talented ballroom dancer.

https://www.legacy.com/obituaries/washingtonpost/obituary.aspx?n=therese-brendler&pid=190710891&fhid=17001

The three bears were sitting comfortably in their living room watching television when they saw a news story about sick bears who had developed severe lung infections.

Some bears became so sick that they had to be treated in hospitals.

They also heard that the same illness had spread to Asia, Europe, the Middle East, Africa, and North and South America.

Papa Bear said, "I wonder why these bears are so sick."

Mama Bear replied, "We must learn more about this disease so that we don't become sick."

Baby Bear looked up and said with a smile, "I know what we can do. We can call Dr. Goldilocks."

Papa Bear took out his tablet and called Dr. Goldilocks.

Dr. Goldilocks answered the phone in her office. "Hello, Papa Bear. How are you and your family?"

"We are all fine," said Papa Bear, "but we have an important question for you. We saw a story on our TV about bears getting very sick and want to know if we might catch the same disease here."

Dr. Goldilocks said, "I saw the same report. There is a new virus that is causing bears all over the world to get sick now."

"What is a virus?" asked Papa Bear. "How does it make you sick?"

Dr. Goldilocks sent the bears a picture of the new virus.

"A virus is a tiny particle, so small that it can be seen only with a powerful electron microscope.

"Here is a picture of the new virus. It is called a coronavirus because it looks like a crown with a lot of jewels on it. The scientists call it the *severe acute respiratory syndrome coronavirus 2*, or *SARS-CoV-2*. The new disease caused by this virus is called the *coronavirus disease of 2019*, or *COVID-19*. These viruses lived in the bodies of small bats for many years but just recently managed to get into the bodies of some bears and cause them to become sick."

"How does the virus cause a bear to become sick?" asked Mama Bear.

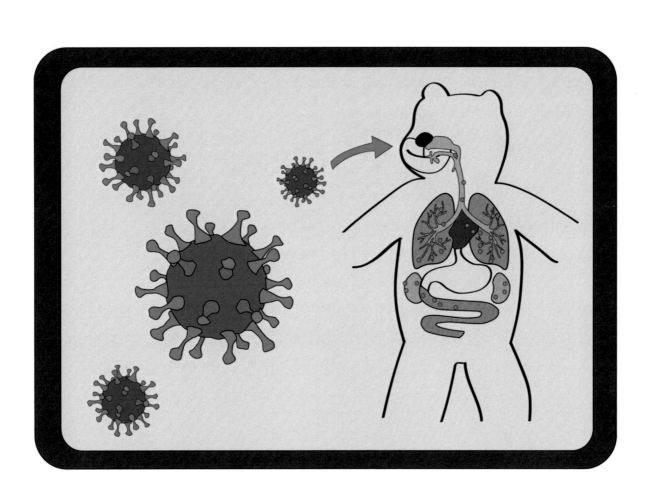

"The virus is so small," explained Dr. Goldilocks, "that it sticks to drops of water, skin, fur, tabletops, clothing, and any object touched by an infected bear. When a sick bear coughs, many viruses come out of the bear's mouth and nose and form a small cloud around the face. If a healthy bear breathes in some of these viruses, they will go to the bear's nose, throat, heart, lungs, kidneys, and intestine."

"Wow," exclaimed Baby Bear, "that sounds scary. What happens when the virus is in the bear's body?"

"The virus causes the organs to become inflamed," said Dr. Goldilocks. "The lungs become so inflamed that the small air sacs fill up with fluid, causing the bear to have trouble breathing."

"Are there other types of coronaviruses?" asked Papa Bear.

"Yes," Dr. Goldilocks replied. "Some coronaviruses cause the common cold. The SARS and MERS coronaviruses caused more serious localized infections several years ago. A different type of virus, called the Spanish flu virus, caused a worldwide flu pandemic over 100 years ago in 1918. I sent you a table listing other common viral diseases."

VIRAL DISEASES

Common Cold	Herpes
COVID-19	Measles
MERS	Meningitis
SARS	Mumps
Chicken Pox	Pneumonia
Cold Sores	Roseola
Dengue Fever	Rubella
Ebola	Smallpox
Flu, Spanish Flu	West of Nile
Hepatitis	

"What can we do so that we do not become infected with this coronavirus?" asked Mama Bear.

Dr. Goldilocks replied, "Here are five things you can do to protect your body from the coronavirus:

"Number 1: Wash your hands with soap and water for 20 seconds several times a day. You may also wipe your hands with a liquid containing 70 percent alcohol.

"Number 2: Whenever you cough, cough into a tissue or your elbow.

"Number 3: Do not touch your face. If you have coronaviruses on your fingers or hands, they cannot get into your body through your eyes, nose, or mouth unless you touch your face.

"Number 4: Practice social distancing by keeping at least six feet between you and anybody else. Your town mayor may tell you not to go to school, church, movies, restaurants, football, or baseball games.

"Number 5: Wear a mask over your mouth and nose whenever you leave your house.

"In addition to these precautions, you should avoid closed and crowded spaces whenever possible and also avoid contact with other bears that are sick. If you follow all of these guidelines, you will greatly reduce the risk of becoming infected with the virus."

The bears started to follow the advice of Dr. Goldilocks in all their activities

One day Baby Bear started to feel sick. She felt warm and had a sore throat and a runny nose. She also felt some pain in her muscles.

Mama Bear said, "I hope you do not have the COVID-19 disease. I will call Dr. Goldilocks and see what she thinks is wrong with you."

Dr. Goldilocks said, "Thank you for calling and telling me about Baby Bear's symptoms. I do not think your daughter has the coronavirus infection. Please bring her to my office so that I can examine her and do some tests."

Baby Bear came to Dr. Goldilocks' office with her mother. They had met Dr. Goldilocks many years ago and were glad that she had come back to their neighborhood after graduating from medical school and finishing her internship and residency training.

"How do you feel today?" asked Dr. Goldilocks.

"I don't feel very well," said Baby Bear. "My throat is sore, and my nose is running. I also feel warm and have some pain in my muscles."

Dr. Goldilocks examined Baby Bear.

She took her temperature, looked into her mouth and throat, listened to her heart and lungs, and examined her abdomen, muscles, and legs.

She also performed some tests in her laboratory. She swabbed Baby Bear's nose and throat and drew some blood for other tests.

After completing these tests, Dr. Goldilocks said to Baby Bear, "Your nose and throat swab shows that you do not have the serious coronavirus infection. You do, however, have an infection caused by the regular flu virus. I will give you an antiviral medicine to take for the next five days. You should go home and rest for a few days. You should feel much better in a few days. You do not have to go to the hospital."

Baby Bear went home and felt much better after five days.

However, three weeks later, Mama Bear began to feel sick. She developed a fever, chills, and also a mild cough. She decided to call Dr. Goldilocks because she was afraid that she had become infected with the COVID-19 virus.

Dr. Goldilocks spoke to her and was also concerned that she might have a COVID-19 infection because of her cough and a decreased sense of taste and smell. "I think you should wear a mask and go to a testing center near the hospital," she said. "They will do a rapid test for COVID-19 with a swab of your nose and throat."

Mama Bear followed Dr. Goldilocks' advice and went to the local testing center. They swabbed her nose and throat and did the rapid test for COVID-19.

After one hour the results were ready. Dr. Goldilocks called to tell her that the test was positive for the coronavirus. "Since you have a mild case, you do not need to go to the hospital. You should go back home and keep away from both Papa Bear and Baby Bear. You should wear a mask and stay in a separate room to sleep and eat your meals. Please call me if your symptoms get worse."

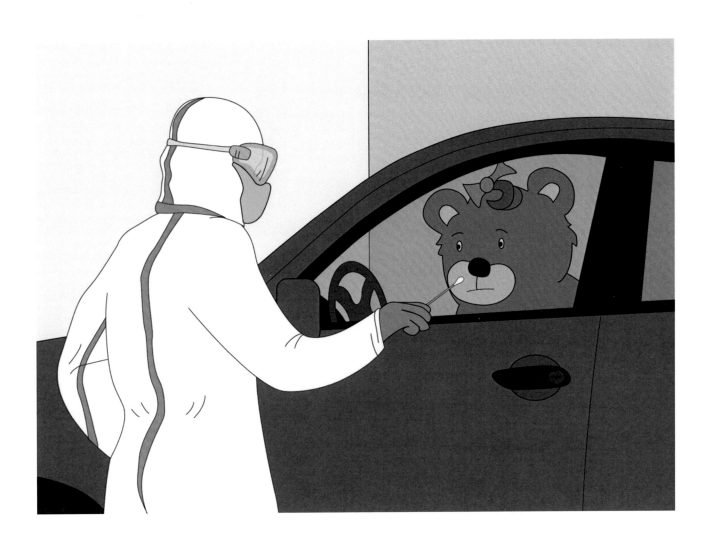

Mama Bear went home and followed Dr. Goldilocks' recommendations.

She spent most of the time in a room by herself.

She let Baby Bear and Papa Bear do all the cooking, shopping, and housework for the next two weeks.

After two weeks Mama Bear felt fine, but then Papa Bear started to develop some similar symptoms. He developed a fever, chills, a runny nose, muscle pain, and a deep cough. His symptoms suddenly became much worse, and he began to have a lot of trouble breathing.

He called Dr. Goldilocks, who said, "Your symptoms are much worse than what Mama Bear had. Since you are having trouble breathing, you should go to the hospital emergency room for blood and nasal swab tests and also special pictures of your lungs that are taken with a CT scanner. You will probably need treatment with concentrated oxygen. I will call the ambulance right now."

The ambulance came quickly to the bears' house and drove Papa Bear to the nearby hospital.

The paramedics drove Papa Bear to the emergency room, where the doctors examined him and did the swab test for COVID-19.

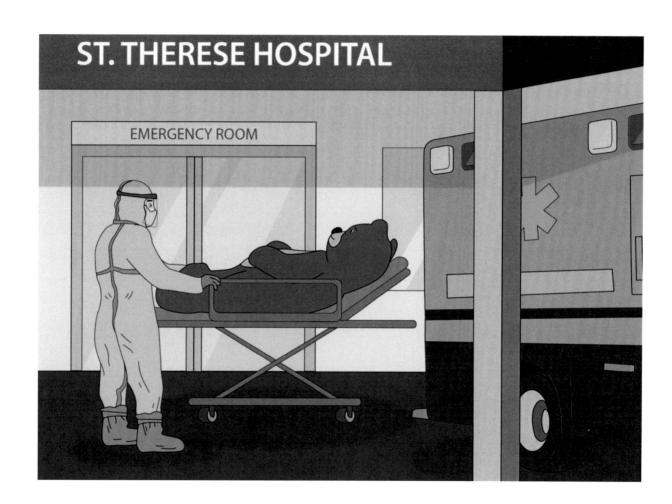

He also had a CT scan that produced a detailed picture of his lungs.

The CT scan showed inflammation in his lower lungs and fluid in the air sacs, a common finding in COVID-19 infections.

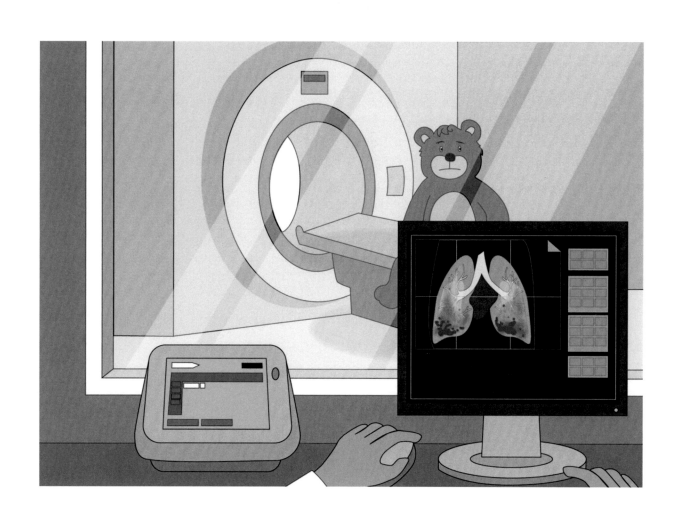

Papa Bear was transferred to the hospital's intensive care unit to receive fluid into his veins and concentrated oxygen from a ventilator. The ventilator was adjusted to give him breaths of 100% oxygen 18 times per minute. He was also given an antiviral medicine and a steroid medication to help reduce the inflammation in his lungs.

Dr. Goldilocks came to the hospital to direct his care. In order to protect herself from the coronavirus, she and all the nurses had to wear special masks, face shields, gowns, gloves, hoods, and shoe covers.

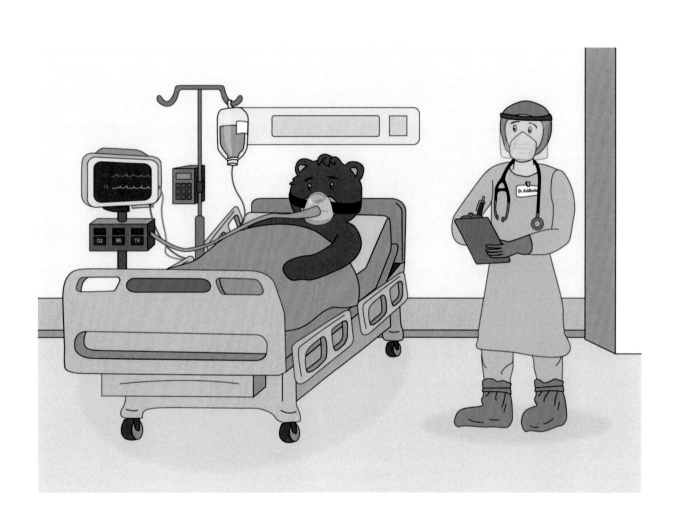

After four days in the intensive care unit, Papa Bear was feeling much better. He was able to sit up and eat. He no longer needed extra oxygen from the ventilator. He thanked all the nurses and technicians for their assistance and encouragement.

Dr. Goldilocks told him, "I am glad to see that you are much better today. I think you can go home in two more days."

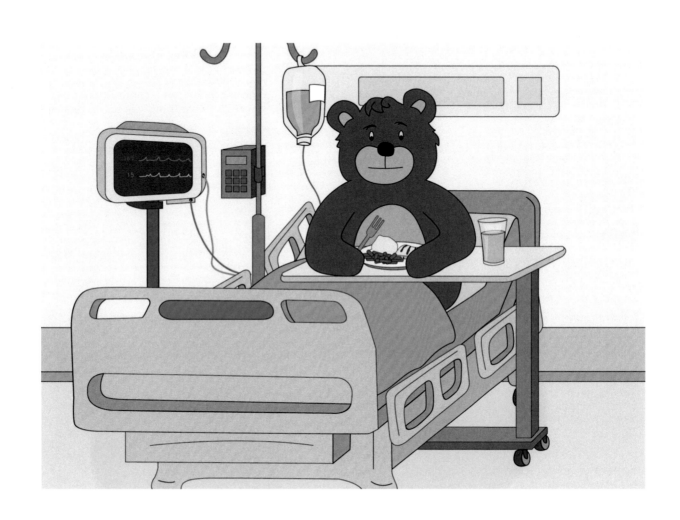

Two days later Papa Bear did feel much better and went home.

Mama and Baby Bear were so glad to see him that they baked a special cake for him.

He rested for ten more days and felt much better every day.

One month later, Papa Bear, Mama Bear, and Baby Bear all felt very well.

They continued to follow Dr. Goldilocks' advice about washing their hands, wearing masks, keeping their distance from other bears, not touching their faces. and avoiding crowds and crowded spaces.

They made sure that they were up to date on all of the recommended vaccines to protect themselves from polio, measles, mumps, rubella, smallpox, whooping cough, pneumonia, and meningitis.

They did not want to have any of these diseases in the future if the coronavirus should come back to their town.

Six months later, Dr. Goldilocks called the bears to give them some exciting news.

"Hello," she said. "I have some very good news for all of you. The doctors and scientists at the National Institutes of Health and many universities and research laboratories all over the world have developed a vaccine to protect bears from infection by the COVID-19 virus. It has been tested in several thousand bears and found to be effective in preventing COVID-19. If 70% of all bears receive injections of this new vaccine, the COVID-19 pandemic will be controlled!"

"That is indeed wonderful news," said Papa Bear. "How do we get this new vaccine?"

Dr. Goldilocks replied, "Please come to my office tomorrow so that I can give all three of you this new vaccine. It is given as an injection in the arm, but the injection does not hurt."

The three bears came the next day to Dr. Goldilocks' office to receive injections of the COVID-19 vaccine. They told all their friends and relatives also to go to Dr. Goldilocks for the vaccine.

Four weeks later the bears came to visit Dr. Goldilocks again.

She told them, "Now that you have received the COVID-19 vaccine, as well as all of the other vaccines, your immune systems should be **just right**. Some bears with multiple myeloma have **too many** antibodies. Other bears with immune deficiency have **too few** antibodies. But all of you have **just the right** number of antibodies to protect you from the COVID-19 virus and other diseases.

"Please come back to see me again if you ever feel sick or have any other medical problems in the future."

The bears felt very lucky to have such a kind and dedicated doctor as Dr. Goldilocks.

Glossary

Antibody — the product of the immune system that fights infections by helping to destroy viruses and bacteria

Antigen — a protein that causes the body's immune system to make antibodies

Antiviral medicine — a medicine that helps the body fight viral infections

Contagious — able to infect another bear with the COVID-19 infection

Coronavirus — an RNA virus that looks like a crown under the electron microscope because of jewel-like spike proteins extending from its surface; it spreads from one bear to another bear and causes them to become very sick; some coronaviruses cause the common cold, but other coronaviruses can cause very serious illnesses.

COVID-19—the name of the disease caused by the new coronavirus, **COronaVIrus Disease-2019**

COVID-19 virus— a new coronavirus that caused several million people all over the world to become very sick beginning in January, 2020; also called *severe acute respiratory syndrome coronavirus 2*, or *SARS-CoV-2*

CT scanner/Computed Tomography scanner—a machine that produces detailed images of the lungs and other organs in a bear's body using x-rays

DNA—a long nucleic acid molecule that contains the code for making all proteins in all living organisms

DNA virus —a virus that has DNA inside its capsule

Epidemic—an outbreak that spreads to many cities and states

Immune system—the complex system in the body that makes antibodies and different types of cells to fight viral, bacterial, and fungal infections

Multisystem inflammatory syndrome in children — a set of symptoms in young bears infected by the COVID-19 virus.

Outbreak—a sudden, localized increase in the number of bears who have a particular infectious disease such as COVID-19

Pandemic—an outbreak that spreads to the whole world

PCR test—a very sensitive method of testing for DNA or RNA viruses

Pneumonia—a severe infection in the lungs

Quarantine—living in isolation for two weeks to determine if the bear will develop the COVID-19 infection

Respiratory infection — an infection in the throat and lungs

RNA — another long nucleic acid molecule that also holds the instructions for making the building block proteins in all living organisms

RNA virus — a virus that has RNA inside its capsule

Social distancing — keeping at least six feet away from another bear to reduce the risk of spreading the COVID-19 infection

Spanish influenza virus — another virus that caused millions of people in 1918 to become very sick

Spike protein — a spike-like molecule that sticks out from the coronavirus membrane surface and helps the virus enter cells of animals and people

Steroid medicine — a medicine that reduces inflammation in the lungs and other organs

Swab — a thin wooden stick with a small cotton ball on the tip

Throat culture—a test with a swab to determine if the patient has a particular type of infection

Transcription/translation— the process that viruses and cells use to make proteins

Vaccine—an injection that causes the body to make antibodies that protect a bear from infection by a specific virus or bacteria

Ventilator/Respirator —a machine that pumps oxygen into the lungs of bears who have a serious COVID-19 disease

Virus—a very small particle that can be seen only with an electron microscope; it contains DNA or RNA and is surrounded by a protein capsule and a lipid membrane.

About the author:

Edward Gale Movius, MD, FACP, FACE graduated from Pomona College with a major in mathematics. He served four years in the U.S. Navy as a corpsman and operating room technician. He attended the School of Medicine, University of California, San Diego, and completed a fellowship in Endocrinology, Metabolism, and Diabetes at the National Institutes of Health. He has treated endocrine and diabetes patients in Maryland, Virginia, and D.C. for forty years. His other children's books are *Dr. Goldilocks and the Three Bears' Thyroids* and *Dr. Goldilocks and Baby Bear's Diabetes*.

TRIBUTE to THERESE GEORGIANA BRENDLER April 6, 1953 ~ October 16, 2018

Therese Georgiana Brendler, 65, of Rockville, MD, died on October 16, 2018. She was born April 6, 1953 in Bartlesville, Oklahoma, and was the fifth of six children born to Joseph Stephen Brendler and Marian Elizabeth Hanley Brendler. Her family moved to New Jersey briefly, and then to Lake Charles, Louisiana where she graduated from St. Louis High School in 1971. At a time when most science majors were men, she majored in chemistry at the University of Texas, Austin, graduating in 1974 with Highest Honors and election to Phi Beta Kappa. She was also granted membership in Iota Sigma Pi, an honorary chemistry sorority, and Phi Lambda Upsilon, an honorary chemistry fraternity. She was awarded the Spencer T. Olin Fellowship for graduate studies at Washington University, St. Louis, MO, receiving her Ph.D. in Molecular Biology in 1982.

She then moved to Rockville, Maryland, to begin a three-year post-doctoral fellowship in the Laboratory of Molecular Hematology at the National Institutes of Health, where she conducted research on DNA transcription. During the time of her fellowship she met her husband, Dr. Edward G. Movius, through the activities of the NIH Sailing Club. She subsequently did research as a staff scientist at the National Cancer Institute, Frederick National Laboratory for Cancer Research in Frederick, Maryland until 2012, where she and her colleague, Dr. Stuart Austin, focused their studies on DNA replication in plasmids.

The P1 plasmid is a small circular DNA element that duplicates itself (replicates) once in every cell cycle of its E. coli host. Replication is inefficient in an E. coli strain which is unable to add methyl groups to its DNA. These methyl groups are added to the sequence GATC in DNA, a sequence that is found several times in the P1 origin of replication. As Therese was expert in isolating DNA binding proteins from E. coli, she set out to see if a binding protein could be found which recognized methylated but not unmethylated P1 DNA. She discovered a protein, now known as SeqA which she showed to bind specifically to GATC sequences which were methylated in one of the two DNA strands (hemimethylated). The origin of the E. coli chromosome also contains multiple GATC sites. Therese was also able to show that SeqA was able to bind to these as well as other multiple sites as long as certain spacing rules which applied to the P1 and host origins were present.

At that time, she and her colleagues became aware that Dr. Nancy Kleckner of Harvard University had found a strain of E. coli that was unable to make a protein which recognized the GATC sequence. Exchange of materials between the two labs quickly showed that the missing protein was SeqA, the same protein that Therese had isolated. SeqA proved to have a most interesting role in both P1 and E. coli chromosome replication control. When a round of replication occurs, the DNA is hemimethylated for some time. This causes SeqA to bind to the replication origin and prevent further initiation to occur until the cell divides and a new round of replication is appropriate. Therese went on in collaboration with Dr. Alba Guarne of McMaster University, to be the first to solve the molecular structure of the SeqA protein and to understand how it binds specifically to the hemimethylated form of multiple GATC DNA sequences in the P1 and E. coli chromosome origins. Her research was published in scientific journals and presented at American and international meetings in France, Sweden, the Czech Republic and Italy. She visited the famous French site of ancient cave paintings in conjunction with one of those trips.

She was a member of the American Association for the Advancement of Science, the American Society of Microbiology, Women in BIO, and the Association of Women in Science, serving as secretary and treasurer of the local chapter.

Since retiring from her research at the National Cancer Institute, she has devoted herself to several volunteer activities including tutoring English to a Korean student, teaching in the science lab at the National Museum of Natural History, information guide at the National Museum of American History, and teaching religious education and serving as president of her church sodality group. She applied the same degree of thoroughness to all of these new activities that she had applied to her scientific research. She prepared very detailed pictures to help the Korean student with his vocabulary. She studied the latest facts on viruses, outbreaks, dinosaurs, and Neanderthal genes so that she could explain material clearly to the students who visited the museum. Her cousin commented that she was very good at giving simplified explanations of complicated principles of science. This ability to organize and clearly present detailed facts was appreciated by the seventh graders in her religious education classes. She devised special Bingo type games to help them learn the new religious vocabulary words. Therese has also enjoyed classical music and ballroom dancing. She and her husband had season tickets to the National Symphony Orchestra concerts and took lessons at the Arthur Murray dance studio, gradually learning several dances steps including the waltz, fox trot, tango, salsa, rumba, and swing. Last month they danced 30 different numbers before judges.

Therese was very adventuresome. She enjoyed sailing on the Chesapeake Bay and Lake Minnetonka. She also enjoyed skiing and traveling to England, Europe, Malaysia, Mexico, and the Caribbean.

Therese's greatest joy, however, was being a mother and participating in the nurturing and growth of her daughter, Christine. She eagerly attended every dance and theater performance as well as every soccer game of Christine during her elementary, middle school, high school and college days. She helped Christine pick out appropriate clothes for school and for Christine's numerous dance recitals beginning at age four and continuing through high school. She and her husband encouraged Christine to do well in math, science and French, and were very pleased that she was able to spend a year in Malaysia as a Fulbright fellow. Therese thoroughly enjoyed a trip to Malaysia at that time. She taught Christine by example how to balance being a mother with having a full-time career, and the importance of continuing one's education and outside interests after graduation. She shared her love for animals by sending Christine frequent clips from the Eagle Cam at the National Arboretum. More recently, she was particularly excited about Christine's engagement and wedding to Evan Sanderson.

Therese was always warm and friendly when meeting new people. She had many very close friends in the church through her association with the sodality, the choir, the Eucharistic ministers and the religious education department. She also had close friendships with the several of the members of the Bethesda chapter of the American Women in Science. One friend commented that Therese taught her what it means to give oneself to the greater community of mankind. She will be sorely missed by all who had the pleasure of knowing her.

Survivors include her loving husband of 34 years Edward Gale Movius, her daughter, Christine Marian Movius, and her husband, Evan Jay Sanderson, her sister Ellen Brendler Kline and husband, Richard Kline, brothers Joseph Stephen Brendler, Jr, and wife, Jeanette Dooley Brendler, Michael Desmond Brendler, and Thomas Brendler. She was predeceased by her parents and sister, Mary Ann Brendler. A Mass of Christian Burial was held at St. Elizabeth Catholic Church, Rockville, MD on Friday, October 26, 2018. She was interred at All Souls Cemetery, Germantown, MD.A Mass of Christian Burial was held at St. Elizabeth Catholic Church, Rockville, MD on Friday, October 26, 2018. She was interred at All Souls Cemetery, Germantown, MD.